I Can Read!

BEGINNING 1 READING

Disney Junior

Fancy NANCY

Nancy's Fancy Heirloom

Adapted by Nancy Parent
Based on the episode
by Marisa Evans-Sanden

Illustrations by the
Disney Storybook
Art Team

HARPER
An Imprint of HarperCollinsPublishers

Ooh la la!

Mom, Dad, JoJo, and I
are going somewhere secret.
"It's a surprise," says Mom.
"Is it the opera?" I ask.

"The ballet? An opera-ballet?"

We pull into Grandpa's driveway.

"Is the surprise here?" I ask.

"Is Grandpa giving me

Grandma Margie's old ball gown?"

"What's new, Frank?" asks Dad.

"Those squirrels keep running

from my tree branch

to my roof," Grandpa says.

"They're keeping me up all night!"

6

"Tell me the surprise," I beg Mom.
"I'm one hundred percent positive
it's going to be *magnifique!*" I say.
That's French for magnificent.

Mom tells me to close my eyes
and hold out my hands.
Mom pours seeds in them.
"We are here to plant a garden
for Grandpa," she says.

"Just seeds?" I say.

"These aren't just seeds,"

Mom explains.

"These are heirloom tomato seeds."

Mom unpacks her gardening bag.
But she brought flower food
instead of compost.
"I need to run home to get compost,"
she tells Dad.

"Why does Mom think seeds

would be a fancy surprise?"

I ask Marabelle.

"Doesn't she know I'm fancy?"

"Let's put our seeds
somewhere safe," says Mom.
"You two can start to break up
the ground like this."
"Yay, dirt!" says JoJo.

"C'mon, Nancy!" JoJo says.

"If I must," I say.

"Life doesn't make sense anymore,"
I tell my sister.

"My own mother doesn't get me."

My shovel hits something.

I clear the dirt away and find

an old wooden box with a rusty lock.

"It's buried treasure!" cries JoJo.

"Open it!"

I tug, but the lock won't budge.

"This is the kind of fancy surprise

I've been dreaming about," I say.

"We must find out what's in here.

Maybe there are jewels inside!"

I ask Dad to help us open the box.

"Sure thing, Nancy-pants," he says.

"Just hang tight while Grandpa
and I take down this old branch."

But JoJo and I can't wait.

"Let's open it ourselves," I say.

I empty Mom's gardening bag to look

for something to help us.

I find a tiny shovel.

We get busy trying to open the box.

A squirrel sneaks up.

He grabs the seed envelope and runs.

"*Sacrebleu!* Oh no!" I say.

The squirrel runs up the tree.

He starts to eat the seeds.

"Stop, *Monsieur* Squirrel!" I shout.

That's French for Mr. Squirrel.

Mom comes back.

She sees the squirrel.

"My seeds!" she cries.

"I'm so sorry," I say.

"Can we go buy more at the store?"

"The seeds are from Grandma's tomato plants," Mom explains. "That's why they mean so much. Heirloom tomatoes are passed down from generation to generation."

"I planted seeds with Grandma
when I was little," she says.
"I wanted to do the same thing
with you and JoJo."

I show Mom our buried treasure.

"My old time capsule!" she says.

"I can't believe you found it.

I buried all my favorite things

in there when I was your age."

Mom pushes a small tab on the lock.

It slides right open to reveal

a fishing bobber,

a friendship bracelet,

and an old tea party photo.

"Who is that fancy girl?" I ask.

"That's me!" Mom says.

"Grandma Margie and I loved
having tea parties together."

"Wow! Look at what else is in here!"
Mom says.

"A few of Grandma's seeds!
They last for years, so you can
pass them on to people you love."

I gasp with excitement.

We can plant them after all!

This is more than a fancy surprise.

It's a wonderful, thrilling,

marvelous surprise!

Mom digs shallow holes in the dirt.

"Seeds, please, Nancy," she says.

I place a few seeds in each hole.

"*Voilà! Voilà!* And . . . *voilà!*" I say.

I cover the seeds with dirt.

JoJo sprinkles them with water.

"When the tomatoes are ready,
may I have a few seeds?" I ask.
"I can save them for the
next generation."

"Of course, and we'll have a tea party
with cucumber and heirloom
tomato sandwiches," Mom says.
"I love you, Mom," I say.
"No one understands me like you."

Fancy Nancy's Fancy Words

These are the fancy words in this book:

Ooh la la—French for wow

Magnifique—French for magnificent

Sacrebleu—French for oh no

Monsieur—French for Mr.

Voilà!—French for see there

Heirloom—something passed down
    from generation to generation